17 party pieces for trumpet and piano

Alan Bullard

CONTENTS

The Associated Board of the Royal Schools of Music

for Mary

A Cheerful Tune

ALAN BULLARD

TRUMPET in B♭

Stately Pavane

AB 2619

PARTY TIME!

17 party pieces for trumpet and piano

Alan Bullard

CONTENTS

The Associated Board of the Royal Schools of Music

for Mary

A Cheerful Tune

ALAN BULLARD

AB 2619

Stately Pavane

Carnival Mood

Melancholy Waltz

Country Stroll

Lost and Lonely

Turtle Boogie

Down-river

The Music Box

Tropical Rumba

Love Song

Echo Fanfare

Barn Dance

Snowy Landscape

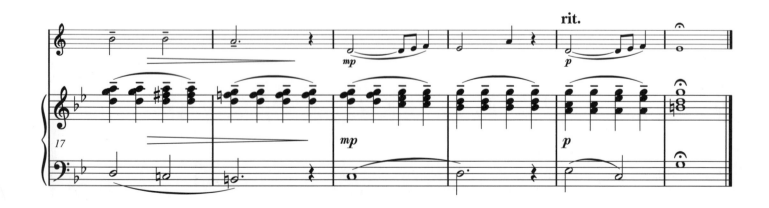

Lazy Day

On the Bandstand

By the Lake

Carnival Mood

Latin-American tempo (♩ = c.160)

Melancholy Waltz

Tempo di valse (♩ = c.144)

rit.

Country Stroll

Lost and Lonely

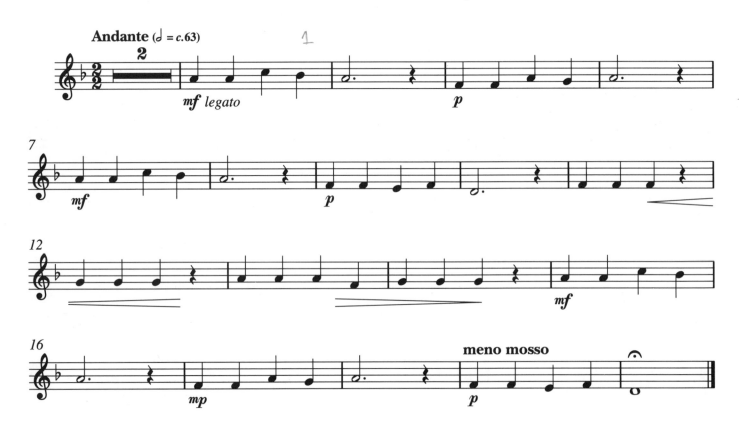

Turtle Boogie

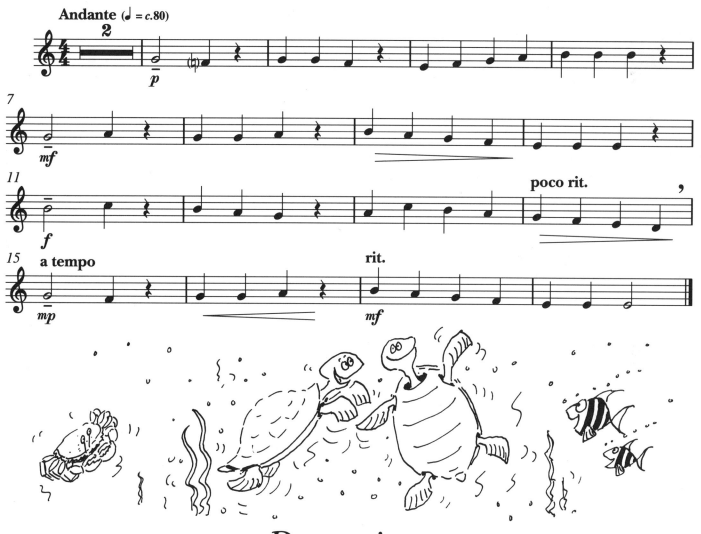

Down-river

6

The Music Box

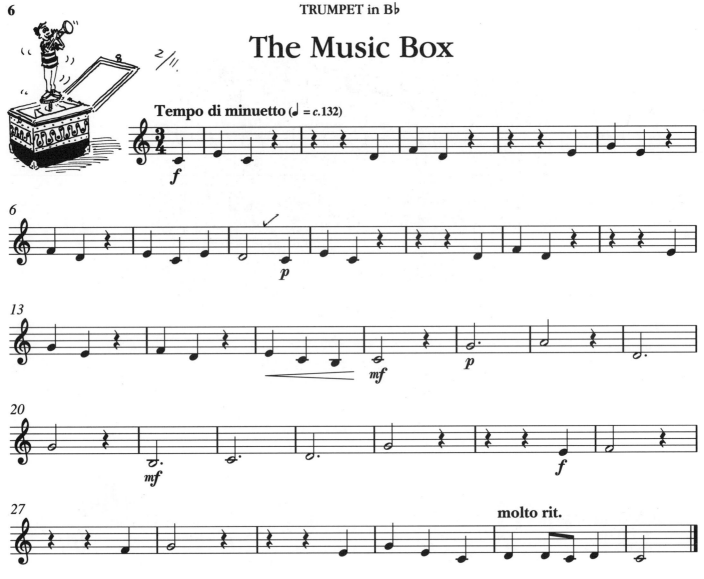

Tropical Rumba

Love Song

Echo Fanfare

Barn Dance

Snowy Landscape

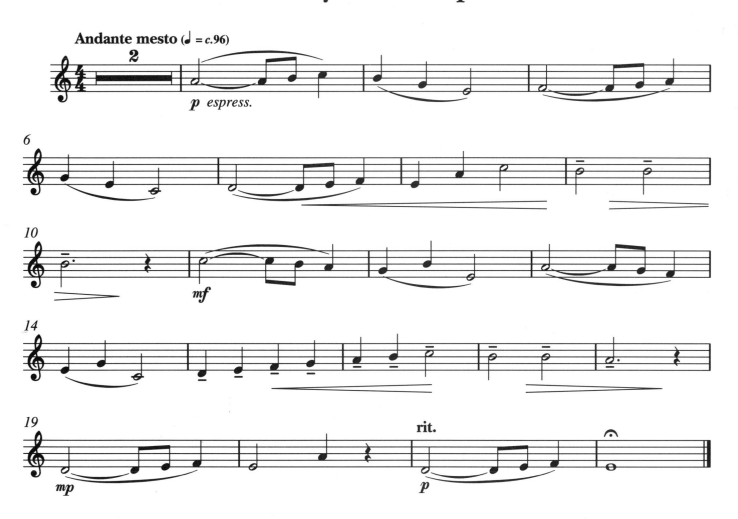

Lazy Day

On the Bandstand

By the Lake